YOU GET
GET AND

WHAT YOU
YOU DON'T
GET UPSET!

Everybody at Molly's kindergarten knew you don't always get what you want.

They all knew that sometimes you just have to be happy with what you get, and you can't get upset about it if it isn't exactly what you were hoping for.

But they
      weren't always
            happy about it!

'Hey, that's **my** favourite colour,' said Thomas.

'**I ALWAYS** use that colour for my drawings!'

'Well, I got it **first!**' replied Harry.

'You'll have to use a **different** one.
You GET what
you GET
and
you DON'T
get UPSET!'

'I need the **tigers** for **my** zoo – all that's left are cows. Zoos don't have cows!' cried Ryan.

'Well maybe this time they can,' said Clara. 'I already have the tigers here for my baby. She gets very upset without her tigers.

You GET what you GET and you DON'T get UPSET!'

'I'm afraid you're sitting on my favourite cushion and not this other cushion that is NOT my favourite,' said Sally.

'You GET what you GET and you DON'T get UPSET!' replied Amy.

Today, Xavier's mum baked cupcakes to celebrate his birthday! Everyone knew which one they wanted ... but they also all knew that sometimes ...

'You GET what you GET and you DON'T get UPSET!'

Sometimes it can be hard to get what you get and NOT get **upset**.

Sometimes what you get is NOT QUITE what you want, but it's close enough.

And sometimes things work out just **right!**

BUT
sometimes ...

'All right, everyone – time for a drink, I think! Go fetch a cup!'

... there's a YELLOW CUP situation!

Everybody knew
the yellow cup was
the BEST cup.

The problem
was, it was
also the ONLY
YELLOW cup!

There used to be more – but now there was ONLY ONE.

And EVERYONE ALWAYS wanted it!

James wanted it
because it was his
favourite
colour.

Amy wanted it
because she said
water in that cup
tasted the best.

No one was sure why
Georgie wanted it – but
she really **did!**

EVERYBODY
WANTED IT!

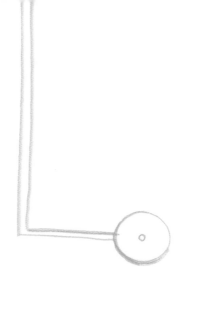

'Phew – what a
big day.

I could do with a coffee!
Hey, that's **my** favourite mug!'

'Well, you know what
they say –
**you GET what
you GET ...'**

'... and you DON'T get UPSET!'